Exploring Antarctica
Continents of the World
Geography Series

Author: Michael Kramme, Ph.D.
Consultants: Schyrlet Cameron and Carolyn Craig
Editors: Mary Dieterich and Sarah M. Anderson

COPYRIGHT © 2012 Mark Twain Media, Inc.

ISBN 978-1-58037-621-1

Printing No. CD-404171

Mark Twain Media, Inc., Publishers
Distributed by Carson-Dellosa Publishing LLC

Map Source: Mountain High Maps® Copyright © 1997 Digital Wisdom, Inc.

Visit us at www.carsondellosa.com

Table of Contents

Introduction to the Teacher

Exploring Antarctica is one of the seven books in Mark Twain Media's *Continents of the World Geography Series.* The books are a valuable resource for any classroom. The series can be used to supplement the middle-school geography and social studies curriculum. The books support the goal of the National Geography Standards to prepare students for life in a global community by strengthening geographical literacy.

The intent of the *Continents of the World Geography Series* is to help students better understand the world around them through the study of geography. Each book focuses on one continent. Information and facts are presented in an easy-to-read and easy-to-understand format that does not overwhelm the learner. The text presents only the most important information in small, organized bites to make it easier for students to comprehend. Vocabulary words are boldfaced in the text. For quick reference, these words are listed in a glossary at the back of the book.

The series is specifically designed to facilitate planning for the diverse learning styles and skill levels of middle-school students. Each book is divided into several units. Each unit provides the teacher with alternative methods of instruction.

Unit Features
- <u>Close-Up</u> introduces facts and information as a reading exercise.
- <u>Knowledge Check</u> assesses student understanding of the reading exercise using selected response and constructed response questioning strategies.
- <u>Map Follow-Up</u> provides opportunities for students to report information from a spatial perspective.
- <u>Explore</u> allows students to expand learning by participating in high-interest, hands-on activities.
- <u>Glossary</u> lists the boldfaced words with definitions.

Online Resources
- <u>Reluctant Reader Text</u>: A modified version of the reading exercise pages can be downloaded from www.carsondellosa.com. In the Search box, enter the produce code CD-404171. When you reach the *Exploring Antarctica* product page, click on the Resources or Downloads tab. Then click on the Lower Reading Level Text Download.
- The readability level of the text has been modified to facilitate struggling readers. The Flesch-Kincaid Readability formula, which is built into Microsoft Word™, was used to determine the readability level. The formula calculates the number of words, sentences, and paragraphs in each selection to produce a reading level.

Additional Resources
<u>Classroom Decoratives</u>: The *Seven Continents of the World* and *World Landmarks and Locales Topper* bulletin board sets are available through Mark Twain Media/Carson-Dellosa Publishing LLC. These classroom decoratives visually reinforce geography lessons found in the *Continents of the World Geography Series* in an interesting and attention-grabbing way.

The Continents: Close-Up

A **continent** is a large landmass completely or mostly surrounded by water. The continents make up just over 29 percent of the earth's surface. They occupy about 57,100,000 square miles (148,000,000 sq. km). More than 65 percent of the land area is in the Northern Hemisphere.

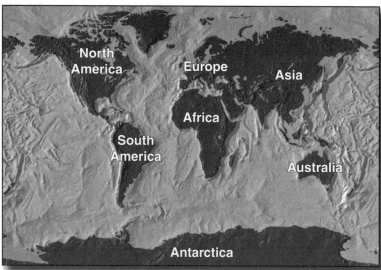

The Continents Today

Landmasses

- Continents: Geographers list North America, South America, Europe, Asia, Africa, Australia, and Antarctica as continents.
- Subcontinents: Greenland and the India-Pakistan area are sometimes referred to as "subcontinents."
- Microcontinents: Madagascar and the Seychelles Islands are often called "microcontinents."
- Oceania: The island groups in the Pacific Ocean are called Oceania, but they are not considered a continent.

How Were the Continents Formed?

For many years, Europeans believed the continents were formed by a catastrophe or series of catastrophes, such as floods, earthquakes, and volcanoes. In 1596, a Dutch mapmaker, Abraham Ortelius, noted that the Americas' eastern coasts and the western coasts of Europe and Africa looked as if they fit together. He proposed that once they had been joined but later were torn apart.

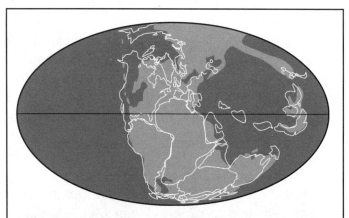

Wegener's theoretical continent, Pangaea, during the Permian Age (white outlines indicate current continents)

Many years later, a German named Alfred Lothar Wegener published a book in which he explained his theory of the "**Continental Drift**." Wegener, like Ortelius, believed that the earth originally had one supercontinent. He named it **Pangaea** from the Greek word meaning "all lands." He believed that the large landmass was a lighter rock that floated on a heavier rock, like ice floats on water.

Wegener's theory stated that the landmasses were still moving at a rate of about one yard each century. Wegener believed that Pangaea existed in the Permian Age. Then Pangaea slowly divided into two continents, the upper part, **Laurasia**, and the lower, **Gondwanaland**, during the Triassic Age.

By the Jurassic Age, the landmasses had moved into what we could recognize as the seven continents, although they were still located near each other. Eventually, the continents "drifted" to their present locations.

Most scientists had been in agreement on the continental drift theory until researchers in the 1960s discovered several major mountain ranges on the ocean floor. These mountains suggested that the earth's crust consists of about 20 slabs or **plates**.

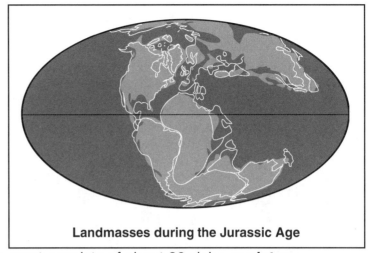

Landmasses during the Jurassic Age

These discoveries led to a new theory, "**Plate Tectonics**," which has become more popular. This theory suggests that these plates move a few inches each year. In some places the plates are moving apart, while in others, the plates are colliding or scraping against each other.

Scientists also discovered that most volcanoes and earthquakes occur along the boundaries of the various plates. Recent earthquakes near Indonesia and Japan along the boundaries of the Indo-Australian, Eurasian, Philippine, and Pacific Plates have triggered devastating tsunamis that killed hundreds of thousands of people. Scientists hope that further study will help them increase their understanding of Earth's story.

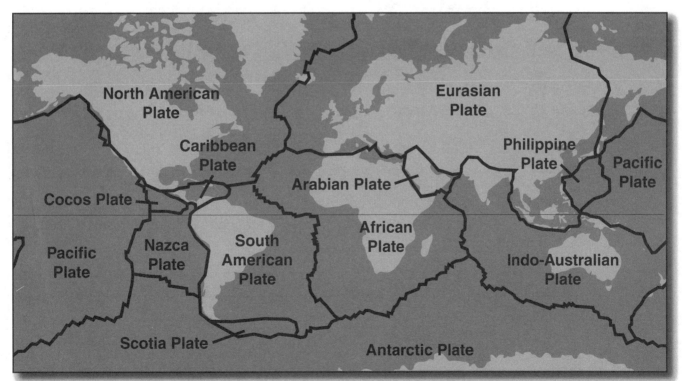

The earth's crust consists of about 20 plates. Plate tectonics suggest that these plates move a few inches each year.

Name: _____ Date: _____

Knowledge Check

Matching

_____ 1. Plate Tectonics
_____ 2. Laurasia
_____ 3. continent
_____ 4. Gondwanaland
_____ 5. Pangaea

a. lower part of Pangaea
b. Greek word meaning "all lands"
c. theory suggesting that plates move a few inches each year
d. upper part of Pangaea
e. a large landmass completely or mostly surrounded by water

Multiple Choice

6. He explained his theory of the Continental Drift.

   a. Abraham Ortelius
   b. Alfred Lothar Wegener
   c. Pangaea
   d. Laurasia

7. The earth's crust consists of _____ plates.

   a. about 20
   b. about 10
   c. about 5
   d. about 50

Did You Know?

Earth is thought to be the only planet in our solar system that has plate tectonics.

Constructed Response

Explain how the movement of the earth's plates formed the seven continents. Use two details from the selection to support your answer.

_____
_____
_____
_____
_____
_____

Name: _____   Date: _____

Map Follow-Up

Directions: There are seven continents and four oceans. Match the numbers on the map with the names of the continents and oceans.

_____ Pacific Ocean   _____ Arctic Ocean   _____ Atlantic Ocean

_____ Indian Ocean   _____ Africa   _____ Antarctica

_____ Asia   _____ Australia   _____ Europe

_____ North America   _____ South America

Continents and Oceans

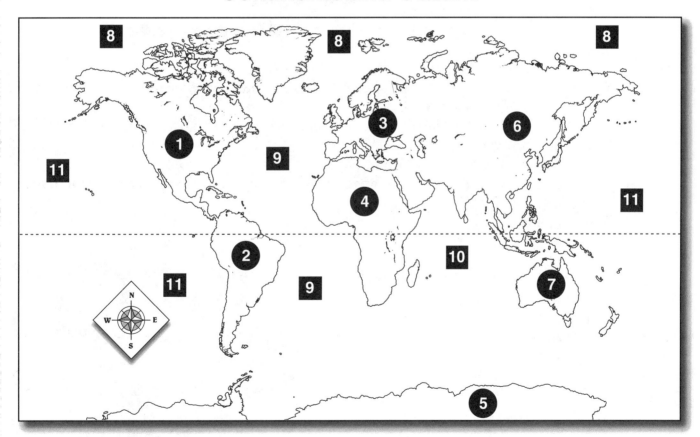

Name: _____ Date: _____

Explore: Antarctica Tortilla Map

Materials

blue construction paper (9" X 12")	pencil	tortilla 8" size
black and red markers (fine point)	scissors	flour
outline map of Antarctica	glue	salt
water	atlas	mixing bowl
white chalk	plastic baggie	

Directions

Day 1

Step 1: Mix 1⁄2 cup flour with 1⁄4 cup salt and 1⁄4 cup of water in mixing bowl to form a modeling dough.

Step 2: Place dough in plastic baggie and set aside.

Step 3: Cut Antarctica from outline map.

Step 4: Trace and cut the outline from the tortilla. Do not discard the scraps, they can be used for other landforms.

Step 5: Use the scraps to cut rough shapes of the southernmost parts of South America, South Africa, Australia, and New Zealand. Then cut out islands for Madagascar, Tasmania, and the Falkland Islands.

Step 6: Place the cutouts on the blue construction paper. Refer to a map from the atlas to position the landforms correctly.

Step 7: Glue the cutouts on the construction paper.

Step 8: Mold the dough on the tortilla cutouts to create mountain ranges for the Transantarctic Mountains, Ellsworth Range, and Andes in South America. Let dry overnight.

Day 2

Step 1: Color in the ice shelf with white chalk.

Step 2: Label landforms, major oceans and seas, and mountain ranges with black marker.

Step 3: Draw in the Antarctic Circle with the red marker and label it 66° South.

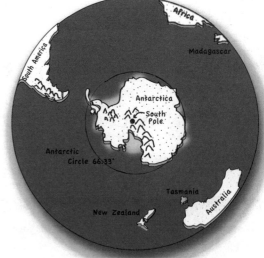

The Continent of Antarctica: Close-Up

Antarctica is the world's southernmost continent. It surrounds the South Pole, which is the earth's most southern point. Its name means "opposite the Arctic." The Arctic is the earth's northernmost region. Antarctica is approximately 600 miles (1,000 km) from South America, 2,500 miles (4,000 km) from Africa, and 1,600 miles (2,500 km) from Australia.

Antarctica is the fifth-largest continent. It is larger than Australia or Europe. It is slightly less than one and one-half the size of the United States. The **Transantarctic Mountains** divide the continent into two regions, West Antarctica and East Antarctica.

Because of Antarctica's severe weather, it is the only continent that does not have any permanent residents. Twenty-nine nations send scientists to several research stations located on the continent. The population of the research stations varies from about 5,000 in the summer to 1,000 in the winter. In recent years, tourists have begun to visit the continent.

It is bitterly cold and almost completely covered by a huge sheet of ice. The ice is often two miles thick near the center of the continent; it then thins out toward the coastline. This sheet contains about 90 percent of the world's ice. Below the ice, the land area of Antarctica is about the size of Australia. Just over two percent of its area is exposed land. Much of the land that is exposed is mountaintops.

As snow falls in the central region, it forces the ice sheet to move very slowly toward the coastlines. Often, when the ice reaches the water's edge, it floats, creating an **ice shelf**. Antarctica has several ice shelves. The two largest are the Ross Ice Shelf and the Ronne Ice Shelf. The Ross Ice Shelf is about 4,000 feet (1,219 m) thick in places. Often, pieces break off the ice shelves and form icebergs.

Antarctica is surrounded by water, including the southern parts of the Atlantic, Pacific, and Indian Oceans. Sometimes, the waters off Antarctica's coast are referred to as the Antarctic Ocean or the **Southern Ocean**. Also along its coasts are the Amundsen, Ross, and Weddell Seas.

Antarctica is the world's highest continent. Its average elevation is over 6,500 feet (2,000 m) above sea level. Its highest point is **Vinson Massif**, which is 16,864 feet (5,140 m) high; its lowest point is on the Southern Ocean at zero feet (sea level).

Ice covering Lake Fryxell in the Transantarctic Mountains comes from the melting of the Canada Glacier.

Name: _____ Date: _____

Outline Map of Antarctica

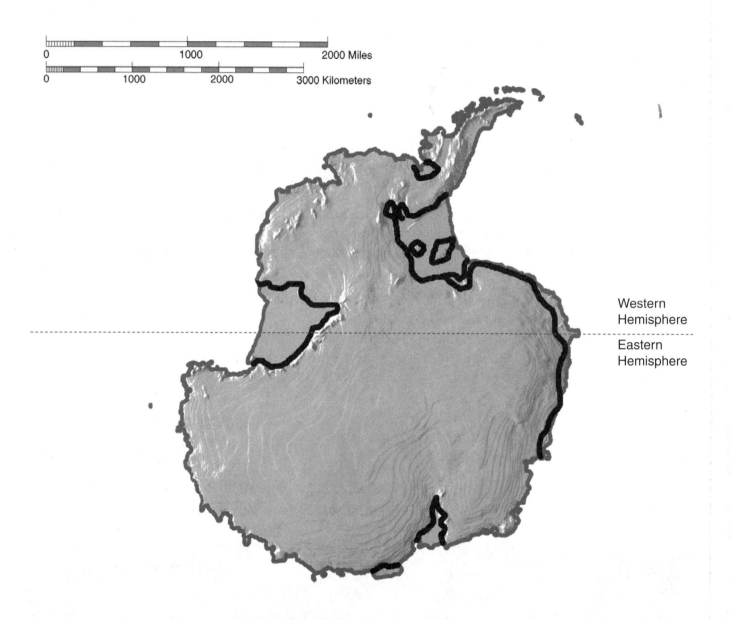

Western
Hemisphere

Eastern
Hemisphere

Black outlines indicate coastline covered by ice shelves.

Name: _____ Date: _____

Knowledge Check

Matching

_____ 1. Antarctica

_____ 2. ice shelf

_____ 3. Transantarctic Mountains

_____ 4. Southern Ocean

_____ 5. Vinson Massif

a. ice reaching the water's edge and floating creates this

b. the waters off Antarctica's coast are sometimes called this

c. "opposite the Arctic"

d. Antarctica's highest point

e. divides Antarctica into two regions

Multiple Choice

6. Which continent is closest to Antarctica?

    a. North America
    b. South America
    c. Africa
    d. Australia

7. What is the population of Antarctica in the summer?

    a. about 10,000
    b. about 50
    c. about 5,000
    d. about 100

Did You Know?

Scientists recorded the world's coldest temperature, 128.6 degrees below zero (Fahrenheit), in Antarctica.

Constructed Response

Explain the difference between an ice shelf and an iceberg. Use details from the selection to support your answer.

_____

_____

_____

_____

_____

_____

_____

Name: _____ Date: _____

Map Follow-Up

Directions: Match the names below with the numbers on the map. Draw the mountain symbol on the map to indicate the location of the Transantarctic Mountains. Label the mountains.

_____ Antarctic Peninsula   _____ Ronne Ice Shelf

_____ Eastern Antarctica   _____ Ross Ice Shelf

_____ Western Antarctica   _____ South Pole

Features of Antarctica

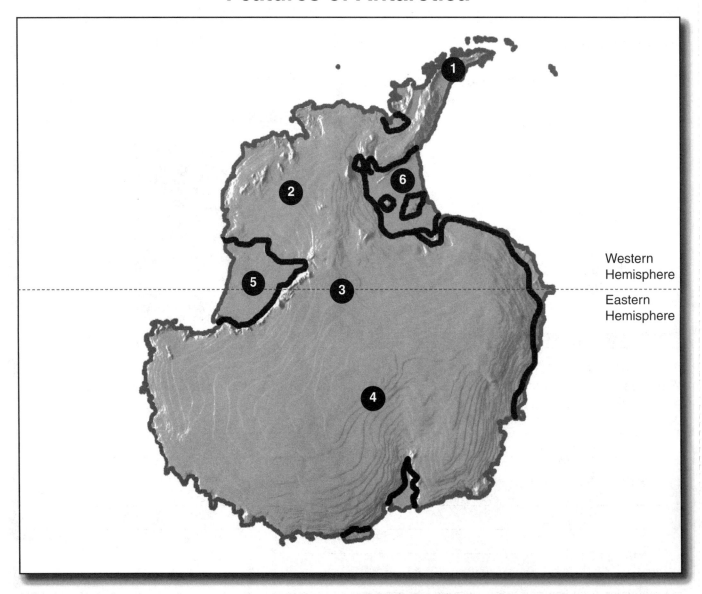

Name: _____   Date: _____

Map Follow-Up

Directions: Match the names below with the numbers on the map.

_____ Weddle Sea   _____ Southern Ocean   _____ Atlantic Ocean

_____ Bellingshausen Sea _____ Amundsen Sea   _____ Pacific Ocean

_____ Ross Sea

Antarctica's Oceans and Seas

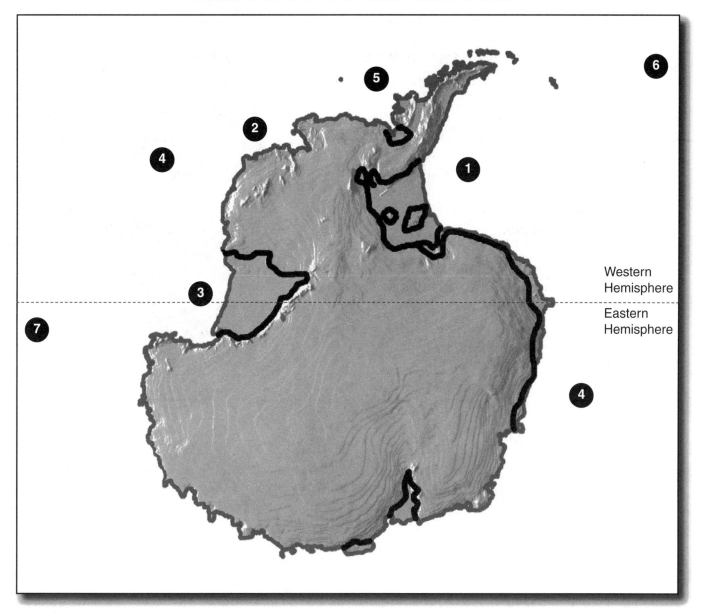

Name: _____ Date: _____

Explore: Edible Map of Antarctica

Materials

copy of outline map of Antarctica	large mixing bowl	white chocolate chips
smooth peanut butter	spoon	powdered milk
measuring cups	can of white icing	powdered sugar
wax paper	blue sugar sprinkles	white corn syrup
table knife	permanent marker	

Directions: Construct an edible map of Antarctica.

NOTE: Make sure that no one is allergic to peanuts, chocolate, or any of the other ingredients.

Step 1: Make the peanut butter dough. Mix 2 cups smooth peanut butter, 2 1/2 cups powdered milk, 2 1/2 cups powdered sugar, and 2 cups white corn syrup in a large mixing bowl.

Step 2: Place the map outline on the work surface.

Step 3: Place waxed paper on top of the map outline.

Step 4: Trace outline on the wax paper with the permanent marker.

Step 5: Place a scoop of peanut butter dough on the wax paper. Press the dough to fill the outline of the continent.

Step 6: Spread white icing thinly over the peanut butter continent form.

Step 7: Use white chocolate chips to represent the Transantarctic Mountains.

Step 8: After discussing the maps, you can eat them!

Antarctica's Climate: Close-Up

All of Antarctica's climates are cold. However, there are differences between the regions of the continent and the seasons of the year.

Laubeuf Fjord and Webb Island in the Antarctic Peninsula

Temperature

- Antarctica is the coldest place in the world. The temperature varies depending upon the season, latitude, elevation, and distance from the ocean. Its average temperature is about 20° colder than at the similar latitude in the northern arctic region.
- The average summer temperatures along the coast are about 32°F (0°C). In the continent's interior, the summer temperatures average between -4° to -31°F (-20° to -35°C). The average winter temperatures stay below -40°F (-40°C).
- The world's lowest temperature ever recorded was -128.6°F (-89°C). It was recorded in 1983 at the **Russian Vostok Station**. The world's lowest temperatures occur in August.

Precipitation

- Antarctica receives very little precipitation. It is the world's driest continent. Most of the precipitation is snow or ice. During the warm season, rain falls occasionally in the coastal regions. The coast receives an average of 10 to 20 inches (25 to 51 cm) each year. The interior receives less than 2 inches (5 cm) of precipitation each year.

Winds

- Winds make it feel even colder. **Commonwealth Bay** is the world's windiest place. Winds often reach between 50 to 90 miles (80–145 km) per hour for several days. Wind gusts of over 120 miles (193 km) per hour are common during blizzards.

Elevation

- West Antarctica is warmer than East Antarctica because it has a lower elevation. The west coast of the **Antarctic Peninsula** has the mildest climates; in January, the temperature rises above freezing.

Interior Regions

- The **interior region** of Antarctica has almost constant daylight in the summer and darkness in the winter. Around December 21, most of the continent has a complete day of light; around June 21, it has a day of complete darkness.

In 1985, a hole in the **ozone layer** over Antarctica was first discovered. Each year between August and October, this ozone layer thins out. Since the ozone layer protects the earth from harmful ultraviolet radiation, this discovery concerns scientists. Scientists fear that the additional radiation will change Antarctica's ecological system and may affect the food chain of the continent's fish and other marine life. The size of the hole has been increasing. This has convinced many nations to reduce the use of chemicals that harm the ozone layer.

Name: _____ Date: _____

Knowledge Check

Matching

_____ 1. interior region   a. has almost constant daylight in the summer

_____ 2. Russian Vostok Station   b. Antarctica's and the world's windiest place

_____ 3. ozone layer   c. has the mildest climates

_____ 4. Commonwealth Bay   d. protects the earth from harmful rays

_____ 5. Antarctic Peninsula   e. recorded world's lowest temperatures

Multiple Choice

6. When does Antarctica have 24 hours of darkness?

    a. around June 21
    b. around July 21
    c. around January 21
    d. around October 21

7. When was the hole in the ozone layer first discovered?

    a. 1982
    b. 1978
    c. 1960
    d. 1985

Did You Know?

Since Antarctica is in the Southern Hemisphere, its seasons are the reverse of those in the Northern Hemisphere. January and February are the warmest months, and July and August are the coldest.

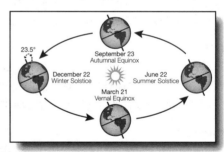

Constructed Response

The size of the hole in the ozone layer is increasing. Explain why scientists are concerned. Use at least two details from the selection to support your answer.

_____

_____

_____

_____

_____

_____

_____

Antarctica's Ice

Over 95 percent of Antarctica is covered with ice. This ice comes in many forms.

Ice Sheet

A huge **ice sheet** covers most of the continent. An ice sheet is a thick layer of ice on top of a landmass. Antarctica's ice sheet is over two miles (3 km) thick in many places. The ice sheet also makes Antarctica the world's highest continent. The ice sheet has an average thickness of 7,090 feet (2,160 m). Antarctica's ice sheet contains about 90 percent of the world's ice. This is about 68 percent of the earth's fresh water.

Ice Shelves

About ten percent of Antarctica's ice cover consists of ice shelves. An **ice shelf** is a large floating piece of permanent ice. It is anchored to the land but extends over water. The largest is the Ross Ice Shelf. It was named for British explorer James C. Ross. It is almost as large as the state of Texas. It is about 4,000 feet (1,219 m) thick in some places. Other major Antarctic ice shelves include the Amery, Ronne-Filchner, and Larsen.

Riiser-Larsen Ice Shelf

Glaciers

Glaciers cover parts of both the ice sheet and ice shelves. **Glaciers** are moving masses of ice on land and come in many sizes. The largest glacier is the Lambert Glacier. It is over 248 miles (over 400 km) long. Most glaciers are slow-moving. The fastest-moving glacier is the Shirase. It travels just over one mile (1.6 km) per year.

Glaciers are formed over hundreds of years. As new snow falls in the Antarctic region, it presses older snow into the ice. As the new ice is formed, it moves slowly from the interior of the continent toward the coastal regions. Glaciers move by the force of gravity and because of the added weight of more ice and snow.

Icebergs

Floating masses of ice are known as **icebergs**. They are formed when parts of glaciers reach the edge of land or when parts of the ice shelf itself break off into the water. Icebergs have many sizes and shapes. The largest one recorded was over 200 miles (322 km) long and 60 miles (97 km) wide.

Most of an iceberg is below the water's surface. Only ten to 15 percent of the ice appears above the water's surface. Antarctica's icebergs drift westward around the continent and northward until they melt in warmer waters.

Pack Ice

Common along the shores of the continent are areas known as **pack ice**. Freezing seawater makes pack ice. It surrounds the continent during the winter months. Pack ice is between 300 miles (483 km) to 1,800 miles (2,897 km) wide.

Name: _____ Date: _____

Knowledge Check

Matching

_____ 1. pack ice

_____ 2. ice sheet

_____ 3. glaciers

_____ 4. ice shelf

_____ 5. icebergs

a. moving masses of ice on land

b. large floating piece of permanent ice

c. freezing seawater makes this

d. floating masses of ice

e. thick layer of ice on top of a landmass

Multiple Choice

6. What percent of the world's fresh water is in Antarctica's ice sheet?

   a. 90 percent
   b. 68 percent
   c. 50 percent
   d. 23 percent

7. How long was the largest recorded iceberg?

   a. over 2,000 miles
   b. over 3,000 miles
   c. over 200 miles
   d. over 500 miles

Did You Know?

Antarctica's icebergs have not caused as much danger to ships as those in the northern Arctic region; there are no major shipping routes near Antarctica.

Constructed Response

Explain the difference between the Lambert and the Shirase Glaciers. Use details from the selection to support your answer.

_____

_____

_____

_____

_____

_____

_____

_____

Name: _____ Date: _____

Map Follow-Up

Directions: Match the names below with the numbers on the map.

_____ Ronne-Filchner Ice Shelf   _____ Antarctic Peninsula

_____ Larsen Ice Shelf   _____ Amery Ice Shelf

_____ Ross Ice Shelf   _____ West Ice Shelf

Ice Shelves of Antarctica

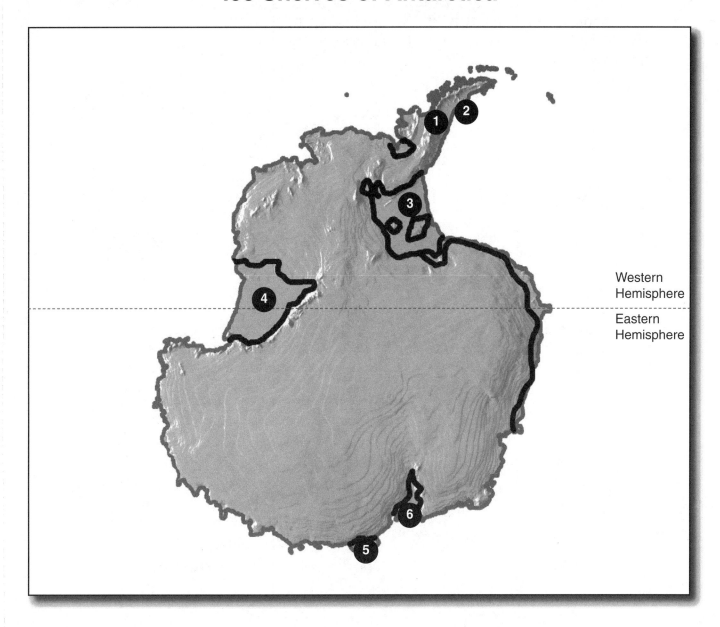

Name: _____ Date: _____

Explore: Ice Vocabulary Study Aid

Materials

Antarctica's Ice reading selection   white sheet of paper
markers or colored pencils   scissors
pen or pencil

Directions: Over 95 percent of Antarctica is covered with ice. This ice comes in many forms. Create a vocabulary study aid to help you remember the names and definitions of each type of ice.

Step 1: Hotdog fold a sheet of paper, with one side slightly longer than the other. 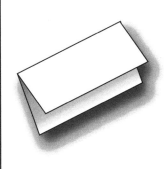	Step 2: Next, fold the paper so that a third is showing and the other two-thirds are covered.	Step 3: Fold the two-thirds part in half. 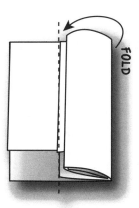
Step 4: Now, fold the one-third part backward to create a fold line.	Step 5: When opened, the paper will be in fifths. Cut up each fold to make five flaps. 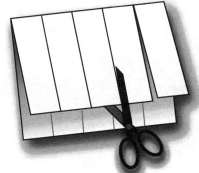	Step 6: Label the tab across the bottom Antarctica's Ice. Write and illustrate the bolded vocabulary words from the reading selection on each flap. Write the definitions underneath (inside of foldable). 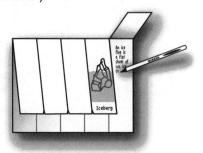

Antarctica's Plant and Animal Life: Close-Up

Antarctica's dry and bitterly cold climate limits its plant and animal life.

Plants

- Most of Antarctica's plant life are simple, often single-cell organisms. Algae, bacteria, fungi, lichens, and mosses grow on Antarctica's few land outcroppings. At times, **algae** grows on the snow cover, creating green, yellow, or red patches on the snow.
- **Seaweed** grows in most of the continent's coastal waters.
- Only two flowering plants, the pearlwort and a flowering grass, grow south of 60° latitude.

Birds

- Forty species of seabirds, including seven species of penguins, live on the continent. Penguins have oily feathers and a layer of fat to insulate them against the cold. Penguins cannot fly, but they are good swimmers and can dive deep into the water to obtain food. Penguins swim up to 25 miles (40 km) per hour and can jump as high as six feet (1.8 m).

Emperor Penguins

- Four species of albatross also live on the continent. The **albatross** is a bird whose body is about nine inches across; however, its wingspan often reaches more than 11 feet (3 m) from tip to tip.
- Other seabirds living on the continent include a variety of gulls, skuas, and terns. They live mostly on the islands and in the coastal regions.

Krill

- **Krill** is the most important animal in Antarctica. It is a small shrimp-like animal that grows to approximately one inch (2.54 cm) long. Krill live in the ocean. Krill is important in the diet of the rest of the animal life in the region. Antarctica's fish, birds, seals, and whales feed on krill. It is often considered to be Antarctica's major resource to the rest of the world.

Mammals

- Six different species of seals live in Antarctica. The Weddell seal, named for James Weddell, an early explorer, lives farther south than any other species of seal. The Weddell seal uses a form of sonar to locate its food. It can stay underwater for up to an hour and can dive to depths of 200 feet (61 m).

Leopard Seal

- Seals were almost hunted to extinction for their fur and oil. Eventually, international laws were passed to protect them.
- Seven species of whales spend part of their lives in Antarctic waters. One of these, the **blue whale**, is the largest creature on Earth.
- At one time, there were over 200,000 blue whales; today, there may be only 10,000. Like the seals, the whales are now protected by international law.
- Eight species of dolphin are also found in the waters off Antarctica.

19

Name: _____   Date: _____

Knowledge Check

Matching

_____ 1. algae

_____ 2. krill

_____ 3. albatross

_____ 4. blue whale

_____ 5. seaweed

a. largest creature on Earth

b. bird with 11-foot wingspan

c. grows in most of Antarctica's coastal waters

d. grows on Antarctica's snow cover

e. small shrimp-like animal

Multiple Choice

6. How many species of penguins live in Antarctica?

   a. forty
   b. seven
   c. two
   d. four

7. What animal was once hunted almost to extinction for their fur and oil?

   a. penguins
   b. blue whales
   c. seals
   d. dolphin

Did You Know?

Penguins feed underwater and do not know how to eat on land. Eating on land is a skill that some penguins in zoos learn.

Constructed Response

Explain why krill is considered the most important animal in Antarctica. Use details from the selection to support your answer.

_____

_____

_____

_____

_____

_____

_____

Name: _____ Date: _____

Explore: Animal Carvings

Materials

reading selection	sand	old nail file
reference books/Internet	water	medium-sized bowl
plaster of Paris	table knife	plain paper
pint milk carton	pencil	glue

Directions: Choose one of the animals from the reading selection. Carve the animal from a plaster of Paris block.

Day 1

Step 1: Pour plaster of Paris and an equal amount of sand in the bowl. Use an amount you think will fit in a pint milk carton. Mix well.

Step 2: Pour enough water in the bowl to make a mixture the consistency of smooth, thin oatmeal.

Step 3: Pour the mixture into the milk carton. Allow time to harden.

Day 2

Step 1: Tear away the milk carton from the hardened block.

Step 2: Draw an animal from the reading selection on the plain paper.

Step 3: Trace the picture on one side of the block.

Step 4: Crave and scrape the animal shape from the block, remembering to turn the animal for a more accurate carving.

Optional: The carving may be finished by coating it with a mixture of glue and water. Mix equal parts of glue and water and paint the carving. After it dries, the sculpture may be painted or stained.

Early Exploration of Antarctica: Close-Up

Two thousand years before the first human saw Antarctica, philosophers and astronomers believed it existed. The ancient Greek philosopher **Aristotle** believed that a huge land had to be in the Southern Hemisphere to balance the then known land in the Northern Hemisphere. He named this unknown land *Antarktikas*, which meant "anti-arctic" or "opposite the arctic." The Egyptian geographer **Ptolemy** believed that the earth was round and must have a large southern continent. He named this land *Terra Australis Incognita*, which meant a "southern, unknown land."

Voyages to Antarctica

- The first person to cross the Antarctic Circle was the British **Captain James Cook**. The Antarctic Circle is the latitude of 66 degrees, 33 minutes south. It is the beginning of the southern frigid zone. During his 1773 voyage, Cook sailed around the continent but did not get close enough to see land. He did see many icebergs and concluded that they would have come from land farther south.

- In 1819 and 1820, Fabian Gottlieb von Bellingshausen, a Russian, led two expeditions to Antarctica. He was within sight of the mainland, only 20 miles (32 km) away, but did not realize his discovery.

Exploration of Antarctica

- The first person to set foot on the continent was an American. **Captain John Davis** arrived in 1821. Davis hunted seals and was looking for a new location to hunt. However, he did not hunt there and soon returned to America.

- Several expeditions from many nations continued throughout the rest of the nineteenth century. British explorer Edward Bransfield sighted the Antarctic Peninsula in 1820. In 1823, British sailor James Weddell explored the region. The Weddell Sea and a type of seal were both named for him.

- French explorer Jules Dumont d'Urville discovered part of the Antarctic Peninsula, which he named "Terre Louis Philippe," in honor of the French King.

- American Charles Wilkes explored the ice coast, which was later named Wilkes Land in his honor.

- British explorer Sir James Clark Ross discovered the huge ice shelf that is now named for him.

- During the last part of the nineteenth century, whale- and seal-hunting crews explored much of the coastline.

- In 1897, a Belgian expedition became trapped for over 13 months when their ship became iced in. Although they had not planned to stay, they became the first humans to spend the winter on the continent. The first expedition that had previously planned to stay throughout the winter was a British expedition in 1899.

- **Robert Falcon Scott** led one of the most famous expeditions to the continent. Between 1901 and 1904, Scott and his men spent two winters in McMurdo Sound. Scott made the first attempt to reach the South Pole. He was not able to reach the Pole, but set a new record for traveling the farthest south.

Name: _____ Date: _____

Knowledge Check

Matching

_____ 1. Robert Falcon Scott   a. first person to cross the Antarctic Circle

_____ 2. Captain John Davis   b. first used the name *Antarktikos*

_____ 3. Captain James Cook   c. first person to set foot on Antarctica

_____ 4. Ptolemy   d. made first attempt to reach the South Pole

_____ 5. Aristotle   e. first used the name *Terra Australis Incognita*

Multiple Choice

6. He set a new record for traveling the farthest south.

    a. Jules Dumont d'Urville
    b. James Cook
    c. John Davis
    d. Robert Falcon Scott

7. Who were the first humans to spend the winter on the continent of Antarctica?

    a. a British expedition in 1899
    b. a Belgian expedition in 1897
    c. an American expedition in 1821
    d. a Russian expedition in 1819

Did You Know?

One reason that people did not believe the theories of Aristotle and Ptolemy was because most people at that time thought the world was flat.

Constructed Response

Long before the continent of Antarctica had been discovered, some people believed it existed. Explain their theories, using details from the selection to support your answer.

_____

_____

_____

_____

_____

_____

_____

Name: _____   Date: _____

Explore: Four Fact Study Aid

Materials

reading selection

sheet of white unlined paper

pencil

scissors

Directions: Construct a four-flap foldable to record information about the early explorers of the South Pole.

Step 1: Fold a sheet of white unlined paper in half like a hotdog bun, leaving one side about one-half inch longer than the other.

Step 2: Fold in half like a hamburger. Then fold in half again.

Step 3: Unfold the last two folds. On the side with two valleys and one mountain top, cut along the three inside fold lines on the front flap to make four tabs.

Step 4: Write the names of the South Pole explorers on the top flaps. Under the flaps, write information about their expeditions. Across the bottom of the foldable, write Explorers of the South Pole.

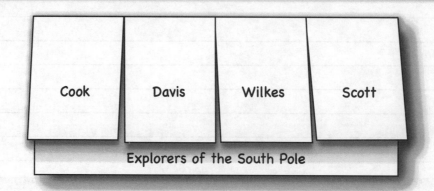

Cook   Davis   Wilkes   Scott

Explorers of the South Pole

The Race to the South Pole: Close-Up

Explorers competed to be the first to arrive at both the North Pole and the South Pole.

First Attempts to Reach the Poles

American **Robert E. Peary** reached the North Pole on April 6, 1909. **Robert Falcon Scott** failed in his attempt to reach the South Pole during his 1901–1904 expedition. **Ernest Shackleton** was a member of that expedition. In 1908–1909, Shackleton returned with his own expedition; however, it failed because of a lack of food.

Amundsen at the South Pole

Second Attempt to Reach South Pole

When Scott returned to Antarctica in 1910 for a second attempt to reach the South Pole, he found himself in a race with Norwegian **Roald Amundsen**. In October 1911, Scott and four of his men left their base on Ross Island and headed toward the Pole. They arrived at the Pole on January 17, 1912. They were bitterly disappointed to discover that Amundsen had been there five weeks before them.

Amundsen arrived at Antarctica in 1910 and began making preparations for the trip to the Pole. He established three deposits of food and supplies along part of the route he planned to take later. On October 29, 1911, he and four men began their trip. They left the **Bay of Whales** on the Ross Ice Shelf just four days before Scott began his trip. Part of Amundsen's success was his careful planning. He planned a shorter route than Scott. He also used dog teams and sleds to carry the men and supplies for the first part of the trip. This helped conserve the men's energy for the return trip. Amundsen and his men arrived at the South Pole on December 14, 1911. They began their return trip three days later. The round trip to the Pole took 99 days and covered 1,860 miles (2,993 km).

When they arrived at the Pole, Scott and his men found a note from Amundsen. It said: "Dear Captain Scott, As you probably are the first to reach this area after us, I will ask you kindly to forward this letter to King Haakon [of Norway]. If you can use any of these articles left in the tent, please do not hesitate to do so. With kind regards, I wish you a safe return. Yours truly, Roald Amundsen."

Members of Scott's Final Expedition

Scott and his men left the following day, after doing some scientific investigations. All of them died on the return journey. Two of the men died of injuries. Scott and the other two men became trapped in a blizzard; they were only a few miles from their food supplies. They died from starvation and exposure to the bitter cold. Eight months later a search party found their tent and frozen bodies. Scott's last entry in his diary was: "... we are getting weaker, of course, and the end cannot be far. It seems a pity, but I do not think I can write more."

Name: _____ Date: _____

Knowledge Check

Matching

_____ 1. Bay of Whales

_____ 2. Robert Falcon Scott

_____ 3. Ronald Amundsen

_____ 4. Ernest Shackleton

_____ 5. Robert E. Peary

a. first man to reach the South Pole

b. led failed expedition in 1908–1909

c. trapped in blizzard; died from starvation and exposure

d. first man to reach the North Pole

e. located on the Ross Ice Shelf

Multiple Choice

6. How many days did the successful trip to the South Pole and back take?

   a. 99 days
   b. 199 days
   c. 89 days
   d. 109 days

7. When did American Robert E. Peary reach the North Pole?

   a. April 6, 1909
   b. October 29, 1911
   c. January 17, 1912
   d. December 14, 1911

Did You Know?

Today there is a scientific research station at the South Pole. It is named the Amundsen-Scott South Pole Station in honor of the first two men to lead expeditions to reach the Pole.

Constructed Response

In your opinion, what were Ronald Amundsen's feelings toward Robert F. Scott? Explain, using at least two details from the selection to support your answer.

_____

_____

_____

_____

_____

Ernest Shackleton: Close-Up

Ernest Shackleton (1874–1922) is one of Antarctica's most famous explorers. He was an Irishman and always had his men's loyalty.

Shackleton was a member of Robert F. Scott's first expedition to Antarctica in 1901–1904. In the spring, Scott, Dr. Edward Wilson, and Shackleton set out to discover the length of the Ross Ice Shelf. The sled dogs died, and the men had to finish the trip hauling the sleds themselves. The men developed scurvy and had to return. Shackleton became too ill to travel, and the other two men had to put him on the sled to pull him back; he was forced to return to England against his will on a relief ship.

Shackleton (in small boat) leaving Elephant Island to get help on South Georgia Island.

First Expedition

Shacketon began his own exploration in 1909 with a group of carefully selected men. They explored and conducted scientific experiments. They explored **Mount Erebus**, an active volcano. They also found a sample of coal from the mountain region. Since coal is made from plant material, it proved that Antarctica had at one time had a semitropical climate.

In October, three members of the expedition set out to reach the magnetic South Pole. They found it on January 18, 1909. By the end of their return trip, they had covered over 1,260 miles (2,028 km) on foot, hauling the sleds loaded with supplies and equipment.

At the same time that the group headed off to find the magnetic Pole, Shackleton and three men started out in a quest to be the first humans to ever reach the geographic South Pole. They crossed the Ross Ice Shelf and discovered the Beardmore Glacier. They reached the polar plateau but ran out of food and had to return before reaching the South Pole. They had been within 97 miles (156 km) of reaching it.

Shackleton and his men returned home in triumph, even though they did not reach the Pole. **King Edward VII** of England knighted Shackleton to honor him for his adventures and bravery.

Second Expedition

Shackleton was disappointed to learn that **Roald Amundsen** had become the first person to reach the South Pole in 1911. In spite of his disappointment, Shackleton returned in 1914 to cross the entire continent by way of the Pole. His ship never reached the continent; it became trapped by the ice and sank ten months later. Shackleton and his 27 men spent many months drifting on an ice floe. When they reached Elephant Island in a lifeboat, they had not been on solid ground for 485 days. Shackleton and five volunteers sailed to a whaling station on South Georgia Island to get help. They returned to rescue the stranded men three months later.

Third Expedition

Shackleton sailed on his third expedition to Antarctica in 1920. While on the ship, he suffered a heart attack and died, one month before his forty-eighth birthday. He was buried on **South Georgia Island**.

Name: _____ Date: _____

Knowledge Check

Matching

_____ 1. King Edward VII

_____ 2. South Georgia Island

_____ 3. Mount Erebus

_____ 4. Ernest Shackleton

_____ 5. Roald Amundsen

a. Irishman who was one of Antarctica's most famous explorers

b. first person to reach the South Pole

c. knighted Shackleton

d. active volcano in Antarctica

e. Shackleton's burial site

Multiple Choice

6. How far was Shackleton from reaching the South Pole when he had to turn back?

   a. 27 miles
   b. 47 miles
   c. 77 miles
   d. 97 miles

7. What did Shackleton discover that proved Antarctica had once had a semitropical climate?

   a. coal
   b. volcanoes
   c. glaciers
   d. ice floes

Did You Know?

Scurvy is a disease caused by lack of vitamin C. It can be prevented by eating vegetables or citrus fruits.

Constructed Response

Explain why Robert F. Scott's first expedition to Antarctica in 1901–1904 had to turn back. Use at least two details from the selection to support your answer.

_____

_____

_____

_____

_____

_____

_____

Name: _____ Date: _____

Explore: Shackleton String Time Line

Materials

reading selection

yarn

metric ruler

plain 3″ X 5″ index cards

glue stick

colored pencils

markers

A time line is a graphical representation of a chronological sequence of events.

Directions: Create a time line for Ernest Shackleton's expeditions.

Step 1: Cut a piece of yarn 1.5 meters long.

Step 2: Using the reading selection, create a time line that shows Ernest Shackleton's expeditions.

Step 3: Place the date of his first expedition on a plain, 3″ x 5″ index card.

Step 4: On another plain index card, draw something that represents that expedition. Also, write one or two sentences that briefly explain the expedition.

Step 5: Spread glue on the back of each card.

Step 6: Place the string at the top of one of the glued backs. Then place the corresponding picture and information card on top of the string, securing the cards to the string. Do this with the other expedition cards. Be sure to put the expeditions in chronological order and leave enough string on both ends to allow the time line to be displayed.

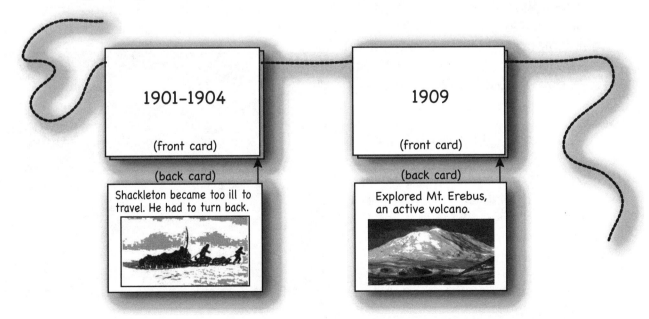

1901–1904

(front card)

(back card)

Shackleton became too ill to travel. He had to turn back.

1909

(front card)

(back card)

Explored Mt. Erebus, an active volcano.

Later Exploration of Antarctica: Close-Up

After Norwegian explorer Roald Amundsen reached the South Pole in 1911, interest in the continent slowed; however, scientific explorations continued.

Fly-Overs

- On May 9, 1926, American **Richard Byrd** became famous as the first person to fly over the North Pole.

- In 1928, Australian Hubert Wilkins was the first person to fly over part of Antarctica. He later made several additional flights over the Antarctic Peninsula.

- On November 2, 1929, Byrd and his crew of three men became the first to fly over the South Pole. Three days later, Amundsen, Italian Umberto Nobile, and American Lincoln Ellsworth flew over the Pole in a dirigible.

Richard Byrd

- Byrd flew over the Pole again on November 29, 1929, and took many aerial photographs during this flight. He returned and took additional aerial photographs during four expeditions between 1933 and 1947. His photographs helped prove that Antarctica was a single continent.

- In addition to Byrd's work, Britain, Australia, New Zealand, America, and Germany all sponsored additional photographic flights.

- Ellsworth and Englishman Herbert Hollick-Kenyon made the first flight across most of the continent in November 1935. They flew 2,300 miles (3,701 km). Their plane ran out of fuel before reaching their final destination, however, and the two men had to walk for 22 days to return to their base.

Expeditions

- Between 1929 and 1950, many additional expeditions visited the continent. George Wilkins and Douglas Mawson of Australia, Hjalmar Riiser-Larsen of Norway, and Lincoln Ellsworth and Finn Ronne of the United States all headed major expeditions.

- The first expedition to cross the entire continent by land was Englishman Vivian Fuchs and his expedition. Their 1958 journey took ninety-nine days.

- The first women to reach the South Pole by land were Victoria E. Murden and Shirley Metz in 1989.

- In 1990, a six-man dog-sled expedition traveled 3,700 miles (5,955 km) across the continent.

- In 1993, Norwegian Erling Kagge traveled alone and on foot 810 miles (1,304 km) across the continent to the South Pole.

Permanent Observation Stations
- In 1948, **Australia** built the first permanent observation station on the continent, and in 1955–1956, 12 nations set up 50 bases for scientific research.

- In 2007, the Belgians unveiled a prefabricated research station that produces zero emissions and is powered by wind turbines and solar panels.

Other Historic Events
- July 1, 1957, through December 31, 1958, was declared an **International Geophysical Year (IGY)**. A major multinational research effort occurred throughout that year's time. By then, the emphasis had shifted from exploration to scientific research.

People had a chance to view the Belgian research station before it was sent to Antarctica.

- A **United States Navy** airplane made the first landing at the South Pole in 1958.

- On December 1, 1959, 12 nations signed the **Antarctic Treaty**, which made the continent a non-military zone for scientific research.

- March 2007 to March 2009 was declared an **International Polar Year (IPY)**, allowing researchers to get the opportunity to work in both polar regions. Over 200 projects with thousands of scientists were completed in a wide range of physical, biological, and social research topics. Previous IPYs had been declared in 1882–1883 and 1932–1933.

Name: _____ Date: _____

Knowledge Check

Matching

_____ 1. Antarctic Treaty

_____ 2. Richard Byrd

_____ 3. United States Navy

_____ 4. Australia

_____ 5. IGY

a. first person to fly over the South Pole

b. acronym for International Geophysical Year

c. made first landing at the South Pole in 1958

d. made Antarctica a non-military zone for scientific research

e. built the first Antarctic observation station

Multiple Choice

6. When did the first person cross Antarctica alone on foot to reach the South Pole?

   a. 1959
   b. 1962
   c. 1993
   d. 1983

7. When was the Antarctic Treaty signed?

   a. December 10, 1959
   b. December 1, 1989
   c. December 1, 1959
   d. December 11, 1959

Did You Know?

In 1935, the first woman set foot on Antarctica. She was Caroline Mikkelsen, the wife of a Norwegian whaling ship captain. Shown below are the Vestfold Hills near where she came on land.

Constructed Response

What effect did Byrd's aerial photos have on the exploration of Antarctica? Use details from the selection to support your answer.

_____

_____

_____

_____

_____

_____

_____

Name: _____ Date: _____

Explore: Antarctica Biography Cubes

Materials

reading selection	cube template	clipart	cardstock
reference books/Internet	glue stick	markers (fine point)	

Directions: Research one of the Antarctic explorers from the reading selection.

Step 1: Enlarge the cube template to desired size.

Step 2: Trace on cardstock for a more durable cube.

Step 3: Write the name of your explorer on one face of the cube. Glue a magazine picture, computer-generated graphic, or make a sketch of your explorer below the name.

Step 4: Organize and neatly write information about the explorer on all the faces of the cube.

Step 5: Crease along the fold lines, add glue, and form the cube.

Option: To create a Bio-cube online, go to the following website.
http://www.readwritethink.org/files/resources/interactives/bio_cube/

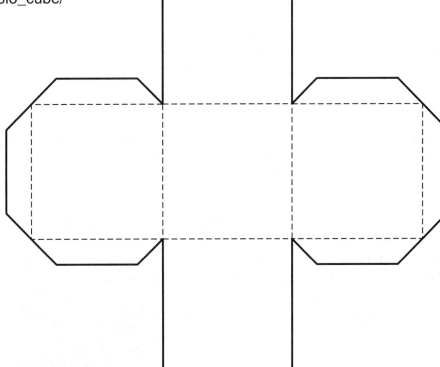

Antarctica's Conservation: Close-Up

During the early exploration of Antarctica, little thought was given to protecting its natural resources. In the 1950s, the growing number of **research stations** began to concern environmentalists. The conservation of Antarctica's environment has now become a major concern among nations participating in research on the continent.

Conservation Issues

Environmental groups such as **Greenpeace** and the World Wildlife Foundation began organizing campaigns to increase public awareness about conservation issues. They argued against the increase of garbage and abandoned buildings left behind at the research centers. As these concerns increased, many nations began cleaning up dumps and shipping garbage and obsolete equipment back to the country operating each base. Another major concern was raised about the construction of any new bases near animal breeding grounds. Most nations have agreed to carefully study the impact on the environment before beginning any construction.

Mineral Discoveries

Scientists have discovered several **minerals** including iron, copper, gold, and silver in Antarctica. So far, the minerals have not been found in quantities large enough to make it worthwhile to mine them. Oil and natural gas have also been discovered on the continent. Environmentalists are concerned that in the future some nations may try mining or drilling for these natural resources. Any mining or drilling would have a major impact on Antarctica's wildlife habitats. In 1991, 31 nations signed the **Madrid Protocol**, which was an amendment to the Antarctic Treaty. This was an agreement that banned any oil and gas exploration in Antarctica for 50 years. Forty-three nations have now signed the Antarctic Treaty.

Tourists

Another area of concern is the increasing number of **tourists** who visit the continent. From the 1960s to the present day, more tourists visit the continent each year. In 2006–2007, a total of 37,552 tourists visited the continent through cruises, fly-overs, and land-based tourism. Since the tourists stay briefly, they have not had a major impact on the environment yet, but fears are that increasing numbers may have a negative effect.

Scientific Research

Much of the scientific research that is conducted in Antarctica is done because of its unique ecology, atmosphere, and environment. These conditions must be protected so the research may continue. One plan discussed is declaring the continent protected as a wildlife preserve and an international park.

Name: _____ Date: _____

Knowledge Check

Matching

_____ 1. minerals   a. agreement that banned oil and gas exploration

_____ 2. tourists   b. substances like iron, copper, gold, and silver

_____ 3. Greenpeace   c. began to concern environmentalists in 1950

_____ 4. research stations   d. conservation organization

_____ 5. Madrid Protocol   e. visit Antarctica by ship or fly-over

Multiple Choice

6. For how many years did the Madrid Protocol ban oil exploration?

     a. 20
     b. 30
     c. 40
     d. 50

7. When was the Madrid Protocol signed?

     a. 1981
     b. 1991
     c. 1971
     d. 1961

Did You Know?

Between 1977 and 1980, over 11,000 passengers made about 45 sightseeing flights over Antarctica.

Constructed Response

Greenpeace and the World Wildlife Foundation are concerned about conservation issues in Antarctica. Explain what action they have taken, using at least two details from the selection to support your answer.

_____

_____

_____

_____

_____

_____

_____

Name: _____ Date: _____

Explore: Antarctica Postcard Packs

Materials

manila file folder

white construction paper

glue stick

scissors

tape

markers

colored pencils

Directions: More and more tourists visit the continent of Antarctica each year. Create an Antarctica postcard pack tourists might purchase to commemorate their trip to the continent.

Step 1: Cut a sheet of white construction paper in half horizontally. 	Step 2: Make a long strip by taping the two strips together. 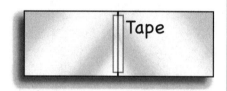	Step 3: Fold the strip like an accordion into four sections. 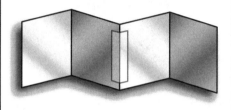
Step 4: Cut out a cover (case) for the postcard pack from the folded edge of a manila file folder. 	Step 5: Open the folded paper and place it on a flat surface so that it forms two peaks. 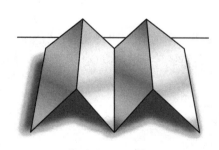	Step 6: Attach the far-left rectangle to the underside of the manila cover. 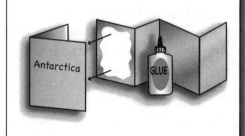

Step 7: Create a colorful picture for each postcard.

Step 8: On the back of each postcard, describe the scene.

Step 9: Title and add an illustration to the cover of the postcard pack.

Scientific Research: Close-Up

Antarctica has become a major site for scientific research. Much of the research cannot be done anywhere else. In 1939, the United States Antarctic Service Expedition under Richard Byrd suggested the building of permanent research stations for scientific study. Two stations opened in 1941, but they were closed a year later because of World War II. Other governments soon established stations to protect territory claims and conduct research.

During the International Geophysical Year (IGY), from July 1957 to December 1958, twelve nations agreed to cooperate on scientific research. More than 5,000 scientists worked in 49 stations. After the IGY ended, twelve nations agreed to continue cooperative research as part of the Antarctic Treaty.

Scientists recovering a meteorite in Antarctica

In the latest International Polar Year (IPY) from March 2007 to March 2009, more than 200 projects involving thousands of scientists were completed at both the North and South Poles.

Presently, during the summer, about 5,000 people conduct research. About 1,000 remain through the winter months. In the late 1990s, scientists from 17 nations operated 36 stations. The largest station is McMurdo.

Scientists

- **Meteorologists** and **climatologists** study atmosphere and weather conditions. By digging through layers of ice, they can study the change of climate for thousands of years. They also have been studying the "ozone hole," which is a hole in the earth's protective ozone layer. The hole reappears each spring and lasts for several months.
- **Geologists** are studying the land structures of the continent. They are also studying the movement of the plates of the earth's crust.
- **Biologists** study responses of animals, and **botanists** study plants' reactions to extreme conditions.
- **Paleontologists** study fossils. Antarctica has become a source of fossils that help trace the continent's history over tens of thousands of years. In 1991, scientists discovered the remains of a previously unknown dinosaur. It was a theropod over 25 feet (7.6 m) long. It lived in the early Jurassic period.
- **Glaciologists** study the movements of layers of ice covering the continent. Other scientists put radio transmitters on icebergs to plot their movements. Some are studying the possibility of towing icebergs to dry regions as a source of fresh water.
- **Ecologists** measure the impact of humans on the polar environment, and **psychologists** study the effects of the polar environment on humans.
- The thin atmosphere allows **physicists** to study auroras, cosmic rays, and radio waves.
- **Bacteriologists** study the behavior of bacteria and viruses in a cold, isolated environment.

Name: _____ Date: _____

Knowledge Check

Matching

_____ 1. paleontologists   a. study atmosphere and weather conditions

_____ 2. climatologists   b. study the effects of the polar environment on humans

_____ 3. glaciologists   c. study fossils

_____ 4. psychologists   d. study plants' reactions to extreme conditions

_____ 5. botanists   e. study the movements of layers of ice covering Antarctica

Multiple Choice

6. What type of unique dinosaur was discovered in Antarctica?

   a. a theropod
   b. a megalosaurus
   c. a barosaurus
   d. a tyrannosaurus

7. How many nations joined together for research during the IGY?

   a. 14
   b. 13
   c. 15
   d. 12

Did You Know?

The McMurdo Station is a major supply depot for the other Antarctic research stations. Each year, thousands of tons of cargo arrive by air and sea, to be sent to the other camps. It has a population of over 1,000 in the summer and 180 in the winter.

Constructed Response

Explain the difference between a geologist and a glaciologist. Use details from the selection to support your answer.

_____

_____

_____

_____

_____

_____

_____

Governing Antarctica: Close-Up

Based on early explorations and research, Argentina, Australia, Britain, Chile, France, New Zealand, and Norway have claimed territory in Antarctica. Belgium, Japan, Russia, the United States, and South Africa have also done research on the continent but have not made **territorial claims**. The **United States'** policy is that all nations should have free access for peaceful pursuits, and it does not support any nation's claims.

Many nations participated in the **International Geophysical Year (IGY)**, which was directed toward a systematic study of the earth and its planetary environment. Twelve of the nations signed the Antarctic Treaty on December 1, 1959, in **Washington, D.C.** It went into effect in June 1961. By 2000, 15 additional nations had joined the original member nations, and another 17 nations agreed to its provisions.

The **Antarctic Treaty** had several major provisions:
- Antarctica shall be used for peaceful purposes only. It forbids any military maneuvers or the building of military bases and fortifications.
- Freedom of scientific investigations would continue.
- There shall be an exchange of scientific information and personnel.
- The treaty does not support or deny any claims to the continent.
- Nuclear testing and disposal of radioactive wastes are prohibited.
- There will be free access for observation and inspection.
- Personnel are under the jurisdiction of their sponsoring country.
- The treaty members will meet to continue reviewing the treaty and to settle disputes.

Many of the decisions of the treaty's member nations have dealt with conservation and protection of the continent's natural resources. Decisions have helped protect seals, managed commercial fishing by creating fishing zones, and established limits and bans on the hunting of some species.

Antarctica has some mineral and oil deposits. However, member nations had concerns about possible environmental threats that mining and drilling could bring. In 1991, the participating nations of the Antarctic Treaty agreed to avoid any mining activities for 50 years.

Name: _____ Date: _____

Knowledge Check

Matching

_____ 1. territorial claims

_____ 2. United States

_____ 3. Antarctic Treaty

_____ 4. International Geophysical Year

_____ 5. Washington, D.C.

a. does not support any nation's claims to Antarctica

b. place where Antarctic Treaty was signed

c. a systematic study of the earth and its planetary environment

d. countries have said they own a piece of Antarctica

e. banned mining activities for 50 years

Multiple Choice

6. How many nations have claimed territory in Antarctica?

   a. 7
   b. 6
   c. 12
   d. 15

7. Countries doing research in Antarctica are encouraged to exchange what?

   a. radioactive wastes
   b. research stations
   c. information and personnel
   d. territorial claims

Did You Know?

Due to the Antarctica Treaty, ten percent of the world is now a nuclear-free, demilitarized zone.

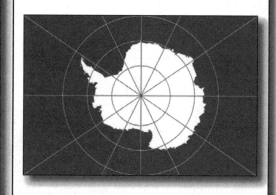

Constructed Response

Explain the importance of the Antarctic Treaty. Use at least two details from the selection to support your answer.

_____

_____

_____

_____

_____

_____

_____

Name: _____ Date: _____

National Claims to Antarctica

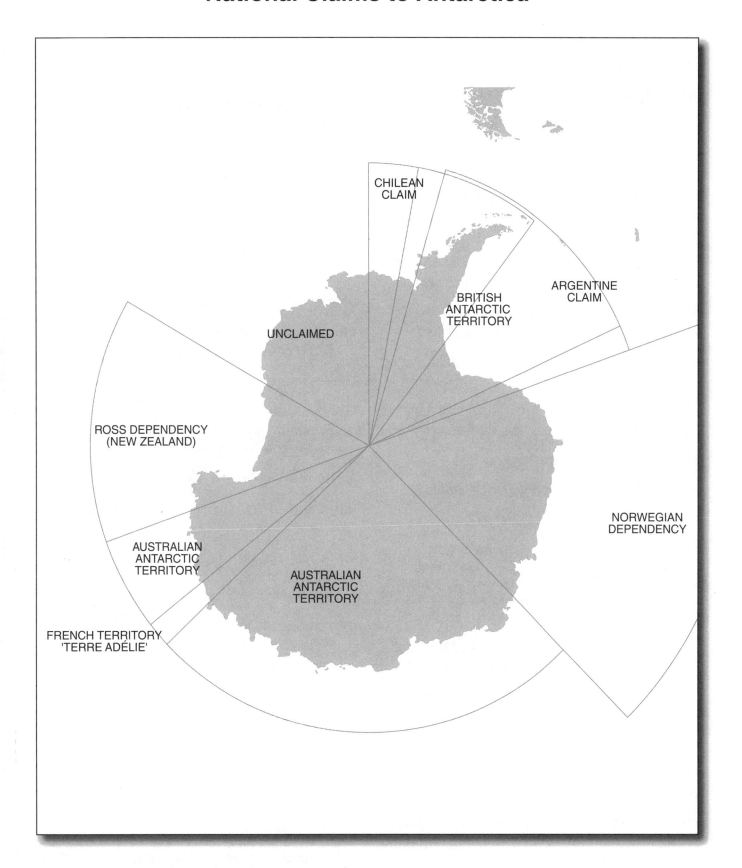

Glossary

albatross - bird with 11-foot wingspan

algae - grows on Antarctica's snow cover

Amundsen, Roald - first man to reach the South Pole

Antarctica - "opposite the Arctic;" world's driest continent

Antarctic Peninsula - has the warmest climates; in January, the temperature rises above freezing

Antarctic Treaty - made Antarctica a non-military zone for scientific research; originally signed by 12 nations in 1959

Aristotle - first used the name *Antarktikos*

Australia - built the first Antarctic observation station

bacteriologists - study the behavior of bacteria and viruses in a cold, isolated environment

Bay of Whales - located on the Ross Shelf

biologists - study responses of animals

blue whale - largest creature on Earth

botanists - study plants' reactions to extreme conditions

Byrd, Richard - first person to fly over the South Pole

climatologists - study atmosphere and weather conditions

Cook, Captain James - first person to cross the Antarctic Circle

Commonwealth Bay - Antarctica's and the world's windiest place

continent - a large landmass

Continental Drift - Alfred Lothar Wegener's theory that the large landmass Pangaea

had broken up and the continents were made of lighter rock that floated on top of heavier rock

Davis, Captain John - first person to set foot on Antarctica

ecologists - measure the impact of humans on the polar environment

Edward VII of England - king who knighted Ernest Shackleton

geologists - study land structures and movement of the plates of the earth's crust

glaciers - moving masses of ice

glaciologists - study the movements of layers of ice covering Antarctica

Greenpeace - a conservation organization

Gondwanaland - the name of the lower part of Pangaea when it divided into two continents during the Triassic Age

icebergs - floating masses of ice

ice sheet - thick layer of ice on top of a landmass

ice shelf - large floating piece of permanent ice that is anchored to the land but extends over water

International Geophysical Year (IGY) - worldwide program of geophysical research that was conducted from July 1957 to December 1958. IGY was directed toward a systematic study of the earth and its planetary environment.

International Polar Year (IPY) - opportunity to study both polar regions from March 2007 to March 2009 when over 200 projects with thousands of scientists were completed

interior region of Antarctica - has almost constant daylight in the summer

krill - small shrimp-like animal

Laurasia - the name of the upper part of Pangaea when it divided into two continents during the Triassic Age

Madrid Protocol - an amendment to the Antarctic Treaty signed by nations in 1991 to ban oil and gas exploration in Antarctica for 50 years

meteorologists - study atmosphere and weather conditions

Mount Erebus - active volcano in Antarctica

ozone layer - protects the earth from harmful rays

pack ice - freezing seawater around the continent of Antarctica makes this

paleontologists - study fossils

Pangaea - ancient landmass believed to have broken up to form today's continents

Peary , Robert E. - first man to reach the North Pole

physicists - study auroras, cosmic rays, and radio waves

plates - large slabs of Earth's crust

Plate Tectonics - theory suggesting that plates move a few inches each year

psychologists - study the effects of the polar environment on humans

Ptolemy - first used the name *Terra Australis Incognita*

research station - place where scientists study the Antarctic; the number of stations became a concern for environmentalists in 1950

Russian Vostok Station - in 1983, recorded world's lowest temperatures

Scott, Robert Falcon - made first attempt to reach the South Pole

seaweed - grows in most of Antarctica's coastal waters

Shackleton, Ernest - led a failed expedition to the South Pole in 1908–1909

ship - the way most tourists visit Antarctica each year

South Georgia Island - Ernest Shackleton's burial site

Southern Ocean - the waters off Antarctica's coast are sometimes called this

territorial claims - when countries say they own a piece of Antarctica

tourists - people visiting or flying over Antarctica; their numbers have increased each year since 1960

Transantarctic Mountains - divide Antarctica into two regions

United States - does not support any nation's claims to Antarctica

United States Navy - one of their airplanes made the first landing at the South Pole in 1958

Vinson Massif - Antarctica's highest point

Washington, D.C. - place where Antarctic Treaty was signed

World Wildlife Foundation - a conservation organization

Answer Keys

The Continents
Knowledge Check (p. 4)
Matching
1. c   2. d   3. e   4. a   5. b
Multiple Choice
6. b   7. a
Constructed Response
The earth's crust consists of 20 plates. Plate tectonics suggest that these plates move a few inches each year. Over time the plates have moved to their present positions.
Map Follow Up (p. 5)
1. North America   2. South America
3. Europe   4. Africa
5. Antarctica   6. Asia
7. Australia   8. Arctic Ocean
9. Atlantic Ocean   10. Indian Ocean
11. Pacific Ocean

The Continent of Antarctica
Knowledge Check (p. 9)
Matching
1. c 2. a 3. e 4. b 5. d
Multiple Choice
6. b 7. c
Constructed Response
An iceberg is smaller than an ice shelf. An iceberg is a floating piece of ice that is not connected to anything else. An ice shelf is still attached to land. Actually, the ice that breaks off the ice shelf is considered an iceberg.
Map Follow Up (p. 10)
1. Antarctic Peninsula   2. Western Antarctica
3. South Pole   4. Eastern Antarctica
5. Ross Ice Shelf   6. Ronne Ice Shelf
Map Follow (p. 11)
1. Weddle Sea   2. Amundsen Sea
3. Ross Sea   4. Southern Ocean
5. Bellingshausen Sea   6. Atlantic Ocean
7. Pacific Ocean

Antarctica's Climate
Knowledge Check (p. 14)
Matching
1. a   2. e   3. d   4. b   5. c
Multiple Choice
6. a   7. d
Constructed Response
The ozone layer protects the earth from harmful ultraviolet radiation. Scientists fear that the additional radiation will change Antarctica's ecological system and may affect the food chain of the continent's fish and other marine life.

Antarctica's Ice
Knowledge Check (p. 16)
Matching
1. c   2. e   3. a   4. b   5. d
Multiple Choice
6. b   7. c
Constructed Response
The Lambert Glacier is the largest glacier. It is 248 miles long. The Shirase is the fastest-moving glacier. It travels just over one mile per year.
Map Follow Up (p. 17)
1. Antarctic Peninsula   2. Larsen Ice Shelf
3. Ronne-Filchner Ice Shelf 4. Ross Ice Shelf
5. West Ice Shelf   6. Amery Ice Shelf

Antarctica's Plant and Animal Life
Knowledge Check (p. 20)
Matching
1. d   2. e   3. b   4. a   5. c
Multiple Choice
6. b   7. c
Constructed Response
Krill is important in the diet of the rest of the animal life in the region. Antarctica's fish, birds, seals, and whales all feed on krill. It is often considered to be Antarctica's major resource to the rest of the world.

Early Exploration of Antarctica
Knowledge Check (p. 23)
Matching
1. d   2. c   3. a   4. e   5. b
Multiple Choice
6. d   7. b
Constructed Response
Aristotle and Ptolemy both believed that there was a huge unknown land in the Southern Hemisphere. Aristotle named it *Antarktikos,* and Ptolemy named it *Terra Australis Incognita.*

The Race to the South Pole
Knowledge Check (p. 26)
Matching
1. e   2. c   3. a   4. b   5. d
Multiple Choice
6. a   7. a
Constructed Response
Answers will vary. More than likely, Amunden wished him the best of luck based on the letter he left for him.

Ernest Shackleton
Knowledge Check (p. 28)
Matching
1. c   2. e   3. d   4. a   5. b
Multiple Choice
6. d   7. a
Constructed Response
Robert F. Scott's first expedition had to turn back for several reasons. The sled dogs died, the men developed scurvy, and Shackleton became too ill to travel. The other men had to pull him on a sled.

Later Exploration of Antarctica
Knowledge Check (p. 32)
Matching
1. d   2. a   3. c   4. e   5. b
Multiple Choice
6. c   7. c
Constructed Response
Byrd's aerial photos helped prove that Antarctica was a single continent. He took aerial photographs during four expeditions between 1933 and 1947.

Antarctica's Conservation
Knowledge Check (p. 35)
Matching
1. b   2. e   3. d   4. c   5. a
Multiple Choice
6. d   7. b
Constructed Response
They were concerned about the construction of any new bases near animal breeding grounds. They were concerned about the increasing number of tourists who visit the continent. They campaigned to bring these issues to the public's attention. Also, both groups argued against the increase of garbage and abandoned buildings left behind at the research centers.

Scientific Research
Knowledge Check (p. 38)
Matching
1. c   2. a   3. e   4. b   5. d
Multiple Choice
6. a   7. d
Constructed Response
A geologist studies the land structures of the continent. They also study the movement of the plates of the earth's crust. A glaciologist studies the movements of layers of ice covering the continent. They also plot the movement of icebergs. Some are studying the possibility of towing icebergs to dry regions as a source of fresh water.

Governing Antarctica
Knowledge Check (p. 40)
Matching
1. d   2. a   3. e   4. c   5. b
Multiple Choice
6. a   7. c
Constructed Response
Many of the decisions of the treaty's member nations have dealt with conservation and protection of the continent's natural resources. Decisions have helped protect seals, managed commercial fishing by creating fishing zones, and established limits and bans on the hunting of some species. It created a military-free zone and stopped any mining or drilling for 50 years.

Bibliography

Antarctica. Evan-Moor Educational Publishers, 2011.

Baines, John. *Antarctica* (The Continents Series). Hodder Wayland, 1997.

Billings, Henry. *Antarctica* (Enchantment of the World Series). Children's Press, 1994.

Fine, Jil. *The Shackleton Expedition.* Children's Press, 2002.

Friedman, Mel. *Antarctica.* Scholastic Library Publishing, 2009.

George, Michael. *Antarctica: Land of Endless Water* (Life on Earth Series). Creative Paperbacks, 2002.

George, Michael. *Antarctica: Land of Endless Winter* (Life on Earth Series). Creative Education, 2001.

Hackwell, W. John. *Desert of Ice: Life and Work in Antarctica.* Atheneum, 1991.

Harrington, Lyn. *The Polar Regions, Earth's Frontiers.* Thomas Nelson Inc., 1973.

Loves, June. *Antarctica: Plants and Animals* (Discovering Antarctica Series). Chelsea House Pub., 2002.

Loves, June. *Antarctica: The Future* (Discovering Antarctica Series). Chelsea House Pub., 2002.

Loves, June. *Antarctica: The Land* (Discovering Antarctica Series). Chelsea House Pub., 2002.

Loves, June. *Antarctica: The People* (Discovering Antarctica Series). Chelsea House Pub., 2002.

McMillian, Bruce. *Summer Ice: Life Along the Antarctica Peninsula.* Houghton Mifflin Co., 1995.

Nicholson, John. *The Cruelest Place on Earth: Stories from Antarctica* (True Stories Series). Allen and Unwin, Limited, 1996.

Petersen, David A. *Antarctica* (True Books: Continents Series). Children's Press, 1999.

Sayre, April Pulley. *Antarctica* (The Seven Continents Series) Twenty-First Century Books, 1998.

Schlensinger, Arthur. *Race for the South Pole: The Antarctica Challenge* (Cultural and Geographical Exploration Series). Chelsea House Pub., 1999.

Winckler, Suzanne and Mary M. Rogers. *Antarctica* (Our Endangered Planet Series). Lerner Publishing Group, 1992

Woods, Michael. *Science on Ice: Research in the Antarctic.* Millbrook Press, 1995.